The Lion and the Mouse

Jackie Walter and Anni Axworthy

One day, a tiny mouse was
scampering about in the forest.
He came across a huge sleeping lion.
The mouse was so frightened that,
as he was trying to run away, he
ran right across the lion's nose.

Mouse's scampering had tickled Lion's nose and woken him up. Lion did not want to be awake and Mouse's paws were making him want to sneeze.

"Oh dear," squeaked Mouse. "I'm very sorry to have woken you."

Lion was never in a good mood when he woke up. He was so cross that he caught Mouse by the tail and was about to eat him whole.

Then Mouse squeaked,
"Don't eat me. I may be
much smaller and weaker
than you, but I might
be able to help you
one day."

10

Lion laughed. "How could a tiny mouse ever help me?" he roared. "I'm the fiercest animal in the forest!" But Lion thought about what Mouse had said.

After a while, Lion leaned down to talk to Mouse. "All right, you can go, Mouse!" he growled softly with a smile. "You won't be sorry. Thank you, Lion!" gulped Mouse.

13

A few weeks later, Lion was hunting deep in the forest when he got caught in a net. The net pulled him up high into a tree. Lion was furious and his roars could be heard right across the forest.

16

Lion struggled with all his might, but the net just got tighter and tighter around him. The sun soon began to set, but still Lion could not get free.

The moon rose and night fell. Lion was feeling weak. All his struggling had left him very tired and hungry. But still he was caught in the net, and still he could not get free.

The next morning, Lion was just about to fall asleep when he heard a squeak and Mouse ran up on to his nose.

"Can I help you, Lion?"
squeaked Mouse.

"I'm stuck!" cried Lion. "No matter how hard I try, I cannot get free of this net!"

"So I see," squeaked Mouse. "I heard your roars, but it took me a long time to reach you."

Mouse nibbled at the ropes of the net. He started on one side and kept on nibbling until he reached the other side. Then he started again. He nibbled and gnawed until his teeth ached.

"I never thought you could help me, but I was wrong," purred Lion, watching Mouse's hard work.

Before long, Lion was free. He jumped down and licked Mouse on the nose. "Thank you, Mouse!" he purred loudly. "You're welcome," squeaked Mouse. "I'm happy I could pay back your kindness to me!"

About the story

The Lion and the Mouse is a fable by Aesop. Aesop was a slave and a storyteller who is believed to have lived in ancient Greece between 620 and 560 BCE, making this story over 2,500 years old. A fable is a story that contains a lesson. This story explains that if you show kindness and mercy, then kindness and mercy will be shown to you. It also explains that there is no such thing as being too small to help somebody.

Be in the story!

Imagine you are Mouse when you are nibbling the ropes. Are you still scared of Lion?

Now imagine you are Lion. How do you feel when Mouse sets you free?

Franklin Watts
First published in Great Britain in 2015 by The Watts Publishing Group

The rights of Jackie Walter to be identified as the author
and Anni Axworthy to be identified as the illustrator
of this Work have been asserted in accordance with the
Copyright, Designs and Patents Act, 1988.

Series Editor: Jackie Hamley
Series Advisor: Catherine Glavina
Series Designer: Cathryn Gilbert

A CIP catalogue record for this book is available
from the British Library.

The artwork for this story first appeared in
Tadpoles Tales: The Lion and the Mouse

ISBN 978 1 4451 4456 6 (hbk)
ISBN 978 1 4451 4458 0 (pbk)
ISBN 978 1 4451 4457 3 (library ebook)
ISBN 978 1 4451 4459 7 (ebook)

Printed in China

Franklin Watts
An imprint of
Hachette Children's Group
Part of The Watts Publishing Group
Carmelite House
50 Victoria Embankment
London EC4Y 0DZ

An Hachette UK Company
www.hachette.co.uk

www.franklinwatts.co.uk

FSC
www.fsc.org
MIX
Paper from
responsible sources
FSC® C104740